British Library Cataloguing in Publication Data

Randall, Ronne
   Sleeping Beauty. — (First fairy tales)
   I. Title   II. Stevenson, Peter, *1953-*
   III. Grimm, Jacob. Dornraschen   IV. Series
   813'.54[J]   PZ7
   ISBN 0-7214-9558-3

First edition

Published by Ladybird Books Ltd Loughborough Leicestershire UK
Ladybird Books Inc Lewiston Maine 04240 USA

© LADYBIRD BOOKS LTD MCMLXXXVII

Printed in England

Sleeping Beauty

written by RONNE RANDALL
illustrated by PETER STEVENSON

Ladybird Books

Once upon a time, a king and queen lived in a palace with their baby daughter.

When the little princess was born, the good fairies of the kingdom each gave her a special gift. One gave her beauty. Another gave her happiness and a third fairy gave her a kind heart.

But there was one wicked fairy in the kingdom. She would not give the princess a gift. Instead she cast an evil spell. ''When the princess is fifteen years old,'' she said, ''she will prick her finger on a spinning wheel and fall asleep for ever.''

The king and queen were very frightened. They ordered that every spinning wheel in the kingdom should be broken up and thrown away.

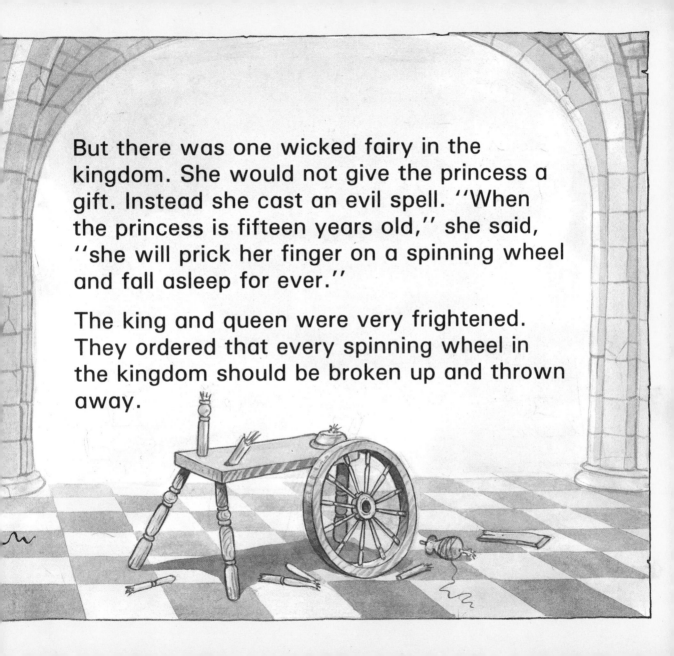

As the years passed the princess grew into a lovely young girl. She had all of the good fairies' gifts. She was beautiful, kind, and filled with joy.

On the morning of her fifteenth birthday, the princess decided to take a walk through the palace.

In a high tower, where she had never been before, she came to a room where an old woman sat spinning.

Of course, the princess had never seen a spinning wheel.

"Please, may I see how it works?" she asked.

"Why yes, child," said the old woman, who was really the wicked fairy. "Come in."

As soon as the princess touched the spinning wheel, she pricked her finger and fell into a deep sleep.

At that very moment, everyone else in the palace fell asleep, too. Even the horses in the stables and the dogs in the courtyard fell asleep.

They all stayed asleep for years and years and years.

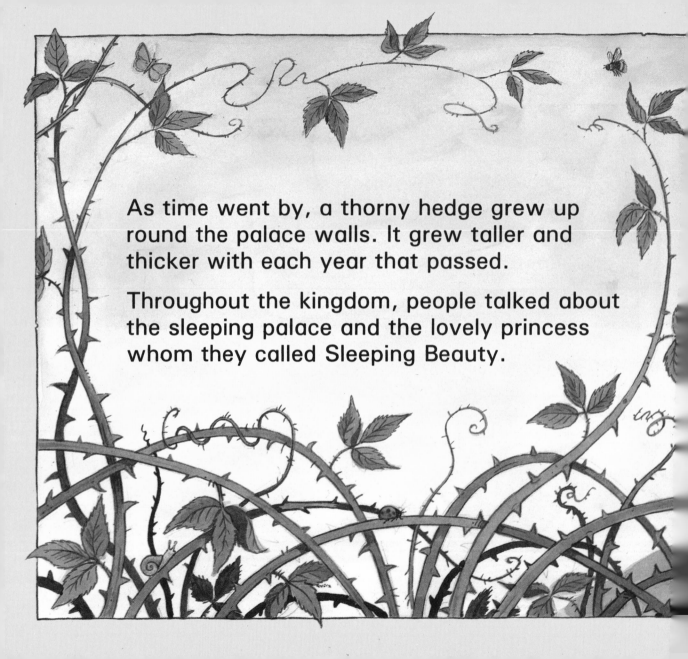

As time went by, a thorny hedge grew up round the palace walls. It grew taller and thicker with each year that passed.

Throughout the kingdom, people talked about the sleeping palace and the lovely princess whom they called Sleeping Beauty.

Every year, young men came to try and climb the hedge so that they could awaken Sleeping Beauty. But not one of them could get past the sharp thorns.

Then one day, after a hundred years had passed, a brave prince rode up to the palace. "I am not afraid of the thorns," he said. "I will climb through the hedge."

But the prince did not have to climb. To his surprise, the hedge parted and let him through.

The prince followed the path to the palace. He went inside and found the room in which Sleeping Beauty lay.

The princess looked so beautiful that the prince leaned down and kissed her.

At once, Sleeping Beauty opened her eyes. The prince's kiss had awakened her!

At that moment, the king and queen woke up, too. And all over the palace, everyone woke up. The horses in the stables neighed and stamped their hooves. The dogs in the courtyard barked and wagged their tails.

The prince had broken the wicked fairy's spell.

Sleeping Beauty and the prince fell in love and were soon married. They had a big wedding in the palace hall with feasting and dancing, and they both lived happily ever after.